Lucky Lady and Other Stories
Femdom Mind Control
Flash Fiction – Vol. 15

S.B.

Table of Contents

Fortune's expensive smile is earned.

Thank you to all patrons of Spell… B-O-U-ND.

I'm lucky to have you with me.

Breaking and Entering

At first, it was just a red dot, flashing against the blackness of the 21.5 Inches Full HD computer monitor. A simple intermittent luminous spot, nothing special about it. Emmett looked at it, frowned, yet kept looking.

Then, it grew. After twelve consecutive flashes, each one separated by one second, the dot doubled in size, and did it again, following the same pattern. Emmett pulled up a chair and sat before the screen, intrigued not only by the animation but also by what appeared to be small irregular lines trying to emerge from underneath it. It was like Morse code, but not quite. It was difficult for him to pinpoint why it attracted him, so he did the next best thing besides looking for an explanation; He continued to stare, absorbed by the growing spectacle of radiant bliss enveloping the room.

The mid-twenties boyfriend with serious husband aspirations had been warned countless times not to take a peek at his lady's study when she was away. He had listened to them all until that day when the scorching Summer heat did a number on his head and dulled his thoughts to the point of convincing him to do the dumbest things imaginable. Depleting the fridge of all alcoholic beverages had been the first. Forcing the lock of the forbidden division, the second. He would pay dearly for both.

Two minutes went by and the dot was now the size of a tennis ball, or a crimson sun orbiting a galaxy of unintelligible code. Sometimes, he had the fleeting impression of white words in the empty spaces between the lines. He couldn't actually read them but knew they were there, undulating between conscious and subconscious perception. It was all so... fascinating.

Another two minutes faded into oblivion and Emmett found himself discarding his pants so he could masturbate freely. His cock was already hard, the shaft pearled in sweat, responding to glorious infrasonic harmonies from the speakers above. He pumped, and pumped, and pumped, losing himself to everything that wasn't the primal need to stroke until Time stopped for good.

He had no idea how long it had been since he had surrendered to the needs of the flesh when Marcia walked in the room, blonde hair glowing from the recent perm. The surprise had everything to be shocking, but she enjoyed seeing him there, mindlessly jerking his will away without understanding why. She kissed his perfectly immobile forehead and purred:

"Hello there, wanker boy. How are you doing? You just had to see for yourself what it is I work on while you spend all day on the couch, didn't you? Well, what do you think? Oh, sorry..." She giggled. "I forget horny pets don't think at all when they're entranced. Why is it that you lot are so easy to ensnare? Well, whatever... best to let the program run its course now but you should know this: this is how addiction begins so you're fucked. I'll let you cum this time, but it will probably be the last in a very, very long time. You don't mind, do you?"

Emmett mewled as the erection raged on, imminent cum explosion about to paint the room white. Marcia took a step back, grinned, and waited for the fallout. It was glorious, and the cell phone camera agreed.

"Now that you've had your fun, it's time for me to have mine. Clean every drop and then meet me downstairs, pet. We have the matter of your punishment for breaking and entering to discuss..."

Glassy-eyed, Emmett got to work, loving every second of it.

Dangerous

Should you ever get married to a woman with a teenage daughter, make sure she doesn't spend her time learning magic spells on the Internet or you'll probably suffer the same fate as me. Let me tell you all about it.

Janine, my wife's daughter, was a typical spoiled brat used to getting everything she wanted in her own terms. After we got married, I decided it was time for her to learn the value of humility as well as the meaning of the word "no" and so I denied her some of the things she took for granted.

First action was slashing her allowance in half, then came the credit card cancelations. For a couple of weeks, things worked out rather smoothly despite her loud protests that I was a dictator in disguise. Instead of going out all the time to hang out with her friends. I convinced her to spend some quality time studying in her bedroom, or so I thought...

On a Monday morning, I knocked on her door to see what was taking her so long to get dressed to go to college and, when she failed to respond, I opened it only to find out the outfit she was trying on was hardly acceptable. Janine sat in bed, pink half top exposing the underside of her nubile breasts, denim shorts so small I could see her ass sticking out as well. The shiny thigh-high boots were beautiful, but...

"There's no way you're leaving the house looking like that!" I exclaimed. "I can see your breasts, for God's sake! And don't get me started on everything else, young lady!"

The little brunette minx offered me half a smile and replied:

"I'm sorry but I'm going the way I want to go and there's nothing you can say that will make me reconsider. I've taken fate in my own hands and, with a little help from my laptop, I got exactly what I needed to do just that."

"What on earth are you talking about?"

"I'm talking about a spell... dad," she spat the word as if it were poisonous. "A bit of magic that will stop you from ever meddling in my life again. I'm glad you're here. The ritual is done, but I needed to have you in proximity to make it work. Get ready because this is where everything changes! Soon, I'll be the one to boss you around..."

"That's enough." I grabbed her by the wrist. "Stop this nonsense right now! And take off those clothes before I do it for you..."

But she didn't listen. Instead, she started reciting a strange mantra to a pagan deity I had never heard before and the words were as terrifying as compelling:

"Oh, Harbinger of Submission! I have you given you my blood in a pact for the ages. Now, grant me what I want most! Enslave this fool's soul, bind it to my will! Let him become my slave in Your Honor from this moment on."

The echo of her words caused the room to shake, a mystic earthquake that exploded in spiraling, blinding light. And so, it came to be that the black magic, awakened by the natural wickedness she carried within, destroyed me. Before I realized what was happening to me, I was already on my knees, begging to kiss the tip of her mesmerizing footwear while she laughed. I'm still doing it right now.

Now, I know my place. Everything she says is right, whatever she decides for me is the truth. I can no longer live without devoting myself to her happiness, and when she has no use for me, I feel insignificant and incomplete. This cycle of humiliation and control will never end.

May this tale keep you on your toes at all times. Teenagers nowadays are extremely dangerous. I learned it the hard way!

Dark Bride

Deanna looked more stunning than ever as She entered the main chamber of the underground cathedral. Around the walls, dripping candles of an unidentified color filled the air with remnants or arcane magic. The leather and latex dark bride outfit was a long-lasting tradition in The Order, and she wore it with pride. Dressed in ceremonial red and white robes with golden and silver complex embroideries denoting their years of commitment to the cause, all the other women present silently expressed their approval, and so did the dehumanized pets snuggling at their feet.

According to protocol, Alan was already kneeling in front of the High Priestess, completely disrobed, when his Owner-to-be stopped next to him, never looking down. It was the last day the blonde basketball player would recognize his birth name. Sacrifice and rebirth went hand in hand when the mysteries of old called to him. His mouth was slightly agape, in awe before the embodiment of feminine splendor he loved more than anything.

Then, the Priestess, a silver-haired woman in her mid-seventies that didn't look a day older than thirty, raised her hands to the congregation and spoke:

"Sisters of The Order, We are gathered here today to celebrate the eternal bond of control between one of Our superior kind and the inferior creature She has chosen to break to Her will by the power of The Underworld

Goddess. Her Control already runs through his powerless veins, but confirmation is required. This ceremony symbolizes just that - everlasting dominance and everlasting surrender - and so I'll be brief...

"Sister Deanna, is this truly the one You desire to serve You in any way You wish for as long as you both shall live?"

"Yes, High Priestess." Deanna smiled, wickedly. "But of course, and according to The Sacred Rules, My mindless servant will be available to any of the other Sisters whenever required as long as The Exchange procedures are carried out, accordingly."

The older woman clapped once and nodded.

"And you, human piece of property, do you acknowledge before everyone in this room and The Goddess Herself that Sister Deanna is Your One True Mistress and that you will slavishly obey all commands given, never faltering, never trying to escape Her rightful justice or wrath?"

"Yes, I do. I live to serve. Deanna is everything and I am nothing without Her." Alan replied without much of a thought, using the same meek mantra that had been forever imprinted in his mind by The Order's otherworldly hexes.

"Perfect!" The High Priestess clapped once more, radiant sparks exploding from the top of her long fingers like fireworks. "Sister Deanna, Your possession of this drone is hereby confirmed, and the connection you now share is unbreakable! Do as You please with it, but I hope You'll be so kind to provide Us with some voyeuristic delights before You leave us tonight to return to Your chambers."

"Naturally, High Priestess." She agreed. "All Sisters deserve entertainment, and I'm happy to provide them the lustful satisfaction They are eager to witness. Slave, you will now worship My divine shoes and legs until instructed otherwise. I don't want to hear a single word from your lips, or even a fleeting moan. You have no need for sounds, an articulate voice is completely wasted on you. Be the chattel you've been taught to be and show everyone here why you'll never be anything else than that. Obey!"

All orders are final, every piece of property recognizes that. The thing formerly known as Alan dropped to its fours and allowed its thirsty tongue to savor Her divinity. Everything was perfect.

Dear and Sweet Chloe

Tick Tock, round and round goes the clock... You know how it goes, don't you?

So did Adam. These words and all its variations were engraved on his spirit after hearing them so many times. Chloe was to blame. Dear and sweet Chloe, who her loving parents believed could do no wrong in the world.

How wrong they were!

"Killer body and innocent mind," that's how he saw her when they met. The early twenties blonde wouldn't look out of place on the cover of a swimsuit magazine and was easy to fool with. A furtive glance here, a whispered innuendo there and she ready to go. Sex with her was never the problem for the moment she embraced it she never once looked back. No, ramming his cock into whatever hole he decided was the best for the day was never the issue but what came after: It was the nagging, the crying, the possessiveness, and the delusions about the perfect future that awaited them even though he couldn't see it yet. Dear and sweet Chloe had an addictive personality that often exploded at the least sign of trouble and, when something got stuck in her head, you'd better hope it was a good one.

For about a year, Adam did that, standing by her whenever she lost control because it was the right thing to do. He had plenty of opportunities to let go, forget her obsessions and carry on with his life, but he didn't, choosing the stoic misery, hoping to make her smile. Dear and sweet Chloe savored the attention, loving him more and more for it, until the day she woke up convinced otherwise.

"You hate me, don't you? Yes, you do. You always have." She muttered by the bathroom door, aquamarine eyes about ready to cause a flood. "Why do you hate me, Adam? What did I ever do to you?"

"Nothing. You did nothing wrong." He would often remark, trying to avoid needless confrontation as much as possible.

"And yet, you still despise me!" She bawled. "You shouldn't lie to my face! I command you to never do that again!"

Command? He should have paid attention to the time she used that word for the first time for the future was already written in it yet, once more, he didn't. Ignorance is bliss until it turns into folly, and when dear and sweet Chloe once showed up at the entrance of his workplace, reality folded in unexpected ways.

"What are you doing here, dear?"

"Do I need a reason to come visit, my love?" She retorted.

"Of course not, but still... something wrong?"

"Not at all. Everything is perfect. I just wanted you to remember I'm cooking and also to give you a heads up..."

"About?"

"We'll be playing a game tonight, one I'm sure you'll love."

"And what game is that?"

"If I were to tell you, that would ruin the surprise, wouldn't it? Just look forward to it and remember: you'll love it."

"Sure, dear. See you then. Now, if you don't mind, these cars won't sell themselves, okay?"

Chloe smiled sheepishly and left, but the wolf inside was already howling.

Two months later...

"Tick, tock, round and round goes the clock... You know how it goes, don't you?" Chloe grinned as she waltzed along the main corridor of her house.

Yes, he did. She would never have him forget. Dear and sweet Chloe wanted another piece of his mind and would stop at nothing until she got it. Like everything else in their life ever since she had discovered the power of non-consensual hypnosis, his illusion of freedom was nothing but that. He could run around for as long as he wanted, he could try to hide under a bed or inside a closet, but she always knew where he was, and could put an end to it whenever she wanted. The tracking device grafted to his leg made sure of that, and it was the perfect technological compliment to the myriad of triggers imprinted on his fragile mind.

"You're mine, Adam. You'll always be mine. And it will even be better after our wedding, I promise!" She chirped, an irresistible pocket watch dangling from her voluptuous breasts.

Sitting in the darkness of the guest bathroom, he cried when the door swung open.

Her Greatest Fantasy

Rosalee and Jack were about to enter his apartment, engaged in civil conversation. Friends for more than ten years, it had been a while since they were last together, and both wanted to enjoy the moment as much as possible. After talking about trifling subjects such as food and music, the banter had veered into unexpected territory, namely, one's greatest fantasy.

"I'm not going to talk about sex with you!" The ebony-eyed barmaid exclaimed from atop her seven-inch heels.

"Who said anything about that?" Jack shrugged. "If you could have anything you wanted, - or be anyone or anything you wanted - what would it be?"

"If you really want to know, I would love to be a mermaid."

"Really?"

"Yeah, I love the idea of them. They're so cute!" She chirped.

"I can do that." He retorted, adjusting his blue-rimmed glasses.

"Of course, you can!" Rosalee scoffed.

"I mean it," Jack insisted, hands waving frantically as if they had been hit by a sudden jolt. "I can turn you into a mermaid, and I'd love to." He grabbed the magnetic key chain from his bomber jacket and opened the door for her to walk right in.

"If you're talking about hypnosis or something, been there, done that," she said, somewhat bored. "Don't get me wrong, it was fun while it lasted, but I don't want a temporary fix. I want the real thing, an actual transformation."

"And that's exactly what I'm offering you, my dear." His eyes glimmered. She had never seen him her comic book nerd friend so excited, and wasn't sure if she wanted to, but she was curious, at least.

"Okay, let's pretend I bite." she clicked her tongue. "How would you do that?"

"Magic, obviously."

"Obviously..." she rolled her eyes once again, stopping midway in the unlikely scenario they would come tumbling down from their sockets. "Abracadabra and such? No thanks, Jack!"

"Maybe this will change your mind then," he replied, traversing the living-room to the nearest bookshelf. Almost instantly, he produced a dark green leather-bound tome. Unlike what one might expect from a so-called magical book, it was quite pristine in every sense of the word, and even the paper smelled of fresh ink. She wasn't impressed.

"Did you print this yourself?"

"I found it in the attic of my parent's old house. Don't let the clean looks deceive you. This is legit!"

"And why should I believe you?"

"Because I can prove it if you let me recite an incantation."

"You mean there's a mermaid spell in there? What a coincidence!" She giggled.

"No mermaid incantation, but a genuine desire one. If that's really what you want, you'll become one. Trust me!"

"Fine!" She twirled and sat on a black maple, legs crossed. "Show me what you've got, Mr. Magician!"

Jack opened the book and flipped its immaculate pages one by one until he found the spell he was looking for. Though it was written in Latin, but it was nothing he couldn't handle. The melodious words rolled off his tongue and then...

... his jaw dropped when he saw an emerald green and cobalt blue fish tail flapping before his eyes.

"Oh my God, it worked!" He dropped the book to the floor. "It actually worked."

"Wow!" Rosalee smiled from ear to ear. The transformation was magnificent. "It sure did, but why are you so surprised?"

"Because..." Jack leaned against the bookshelf and rubbed his temples. "Because I was just pulling your leg. You were right. I printed the book for fun and... Jesus, how the fuck can this be real?"

"No clue, but if one incantation works, then it's possible..."

"... all the others work, too." He concluded.

She was right, and that changed everything. With a real magical book in hand, there was nothing he couldn't accomplish, no dream he couldn't make come true. Even better, no woman would be able to resist him and if they tried... Countless deviant thoughts crossed his mind in a matter of seconds and most of them began and ended in the word "harem". A beautiful mermaid could very well be the first addition.

"Oh, boy..." She muttered.

"What's wrong?"

"I can almost see your brain working from here... you're not having out-of-control, libidinous thoughts, are you?" She pointed her left index at him.

"I would never do such a thing..." He crouched to pick up the book.

"You were always a terrible liar, Jack. And you're even worse when you're horny. I don't think having you in charge of a real magical book is a good thing. You're bound to do something foolish with it, I'm sure."

"Are you?" His eyes glimmered with unnatural cravings, immediately proving her point. "That's too bad, my dear. I don't know how this happened or why, but know that I know the truth, I'll be uncovering every secret of this tome no matter what, so if you're thinking of snatching it away from me, think again!" He gnarled.

Rosalee reclined herself, using the newly created tail as a natural fan, and asked:

"Why would I think of doing such a thing when you will give it to me, willingly?"

"Are you out of your mind?"

"No. I'm a mermaid and if you remember the lore correctly, we have a rather irresistible trait, don't we? I'll be having the book and your mind, dear. Don't worry. I promise both will be in excellent hands."

Rosalee began to sing.

I Must Obey My Mistress

Jonathan got up from bed and walked to the bathroom, a single idea in his mind.

I must obey my Mistress.

It hadn't always been there, but it almost felt like it, a solitary fixation point to keep him focused on everything else that was to come. If he drifted towards undesirable thought patterns like feelings of insecurity or self-loathing, all he needed to do was take a deep breath, close his eyes, and let the overpowering five words reset his mood.

I must obey my Mistress.

Complying was easy when he knew in advance what he had to do. Direct orders from her lips were beyond any threshold of resistance but, most of the times, his owner liked to play differently, leaving breadcrumbs inside breadcrumbs, tiny morsels of tantalizing delicacies he was to savor when the moment was right. It could happen at any moment and when he least expected, and that was incredibly arousing. He trusted her completely.

I must obey my Mistress.

Jonathan confronted the mirror and it stared back at him with half-vitreous eyes. Not that he could see them. He never knew when he was in trance, responding to an indirect suggestion or simply falling deeper by the sheer act of imagining doing so. Anticipation had a special place in his heart and cock.

I must obey my Mistress.

Recently turned forty, his life had made little sense until the first time he heard her voice. The sweet rasp she added to every consonant was infectious, and all possibilities made sense when she was the one bringing them up. That included simple things like sending her a picture of a white rose every Monday morning or being unable to read whatever she wrote between square brackets [What a good boy you are for me]. There were dozens of examples of her subtle yet completely ravishing control over his life, but he could never remember them all. The most important thing was:

I must obey my Mistress.

After taking a quick shower and glancing at the work clothes patiently waiting by the hanger atop his bedroom door, Jonathan approached his silver laptop, turned the camera on, and stroked. A flashing green light meant he was being quietly observed from a distance and green always meant 'go'. Vigorous strokes dictated his need to surrender and yet the pleasure was short-lived, the sweat on his fingertips coming to a halt the moment she cooed:

"That's enough, pet. Your balls are already nice and full, and we don't want any accidents to happen, do we? Go about your business, frustrated, but with a smile on your lips. If you're lucky, we can do this again tomorrow. If you're not, you must wait until I find convenient to use you again. Regardless or your fate, you know what I expect of you, and that is total devotion. What must you do even if you don't know why or when?"

"I must obey my Mistress." Jonathan drooled, the red light shining before him, telling him hypnotic playtime was over. He stood up, the part of him that made him a man shooting upwards like a bloodthirsty harpoon. The throbbing erection would take a long time to subdue, more than he would ever be aware of.

Still glassy-eyed, he reached for his outfit, got dressed, and walked out the door, immediately hearing a faint giggle from his next-door neighbor.

"Good morning, Allie. I'm also happy to see you." He droned.

"You sure look like it..." She laughed in return.

It wouldn't be the last laugh he would hear that day, but it mattered not for he was indifferent to anything other than the simple sentence that totally controlled the world he knew.

I must obey my Mistress, he thought.

And so must you.

Lucky Lady

Danielle laid down her cup of coffee and confronted her sister, Mallory.

"Alec's birthday is tomorrow, right?"

"Yes, it is." The youngest of the O'Loughlin women replied, plastic bag in hand. It was the same color as her sun-kissed hair. "Look what I got him!"

"A collar and leash? Are you getting him the Pitbull he always wanted?"

"Not quite."

"Turning him into your dog then." Danielle chuckled.

"Yep."

"Good for him. I always said he was ripe for training."

"Oh, I've been brainwashing him since we got married. This is pretty much the final step in your relationship."

"Then what? Getting yourself a new bull like I did? I know a guy if you're interested."

"Actually, I've been thinking of playing for the other team for quite some time now."

"Now, that's a surprise! Who's the lucky lady you're dying to fuck?"

"Her name is Danielle and I just spiked her coffee..." Mallory winked.

The cup shattered in a million pieces, followed by her mind.

No Matter What Happens…

"No matter what happens, always remember the mission. You are our only..."

Hope. The voice of Samantha's mother echoed in her ears as she walked towards the center of the once derelict building, ghostly lights illuminating the winding pathway. She repeated the words to herself to remain focused, something that was getting increasingly difficult now that she was in the heart of the enemy.

"No matter what happens, always remember...

The mission. How could she forget? The Order of Hakat had taken everything from her family. Land, titles, reputation... She had trained for this moment all her life. Their ideals of Female Supremacy were nothing more than twisted machinations of a soul-devouring demon. The false Goddess that claimed to be its embodiment had to die and return Darkness to where it belonged. That was her fate, regardless of consequences.

The corridor ended in a pivoting marble door that slid open as she approached. Beyond the threshold, stood a wide rectangular division punctuated by an improvised throne and a skylight bathing it with blood moon glow. Of all the people that had taken the mantle of High Priestess in the past, Rebecca was the first to forgo any security detail such was her confidence that no harm could befall her.

Samantha half expected to see her sitting regally, right hand holding her chin, sensual gaze beckoning her in. Instead, the dark redhead hid behind the corner of her eye, purple cape dress flowing over her slender legs.

"And you are...?" She purred.

"My name is Francine. I hail from the European Branch. I have come purposely to meet you, Mighty Priestess, so you can lead us and Hakat to undying victory."

"Is that so? Not a new acolyte then but an old one who has finally seen the truth?"

"Yes, that is exactly what I am." Samantha replied. A gust of wind swept her long black hair and though she couldn't see them, she felt Rebecca's impossible dragon wings descending over her.

"I like the sound of that. Do you like the sound of my voice?"

"It is very enticing."

"That is the first truthful thing you have said since walking in. Turn around and look at me."

"No matter what happens..." She thought. "No matter what happens..."

Samantha spun in her heels to face the all-powerful Priestess. Immediately, corrupted jet-black eyes pierced her thoughts and pushed her to her knees. All preparations shattered in the face of true power. "No matter what happens... no matter what happens..."

"What do we have here?" Rebecca grinned. "A mantra? Are you trying to remember something that should never be forgotten? True acolytes only keep their owner's words in mind, not someone else's. You are a liar, 'Francine', but even liars learn new ways and can hope to become whole again. Hakat speaks through me and she wants a word with you."

"No matter what happens..."

"No... matter what happens...."

"No... mat...ter what... happ... ens..."

Mistress comes first. There is nothing in this world and the next more important than carrying out her bidding. Her will is your will. Her enemies are your enemies. All must be brought to heel, forced to accept their natural inferiority, starting with your treacherous family who tried to keep you away from the euphoria of enslavement.

Time to serve.

Relic

The sword rested majestically on the worn-out pedestal, its long straight obsidian blade drawing all the light of the surrounding cave. Eleanor was the first to notice it, dark almond-shaped eyes swimming with tears. The corners of her mouth turned up as she cried out to her companion, long-date boyfriend and soon husband-to-be, Harold.

"It's real! Oh my God, it's real!"

"Why wouldn't it be?" He laid down his backpack on the jagged floor and gave her a condescending look even though he had been the first to doubt the success of their self-funded expedition, long before leaving English shores. "I told you my grandfather wasn't a nut job!"

"But if the blade is real, then that means..." she squealed, enthusiastically. "... everything else must be, too! Honey, do you realize what this means?"

"Of course, I do." He hugged her so tightly he could almost hear her delicate shoulder bones cracking underneath. "We're going to be filthy rich and everyone that ever doubted us will have to lick your shoes and apologize!"

"I like the sound of that..." she beamed. "... but can I just shove the sword down their throats?"

"No, honey, because that would be murder..." He grinned in return.

Still holding on to one another, they surveyed the room. It was an irregular rock chamber, not very different from the dozens they had left behind, rare archaeological finding aside. The Mongolian subterranean network stretched at least then miles east of the foot of Mount Chandmani and it was amazing how no one had stumbled upon it in hundreds of years despite the large tourist hotspot. The gods of old were undoubtedly on their side.

"I want a picture, okay?" She escaped his embrace to inspect the blade. The item before her was but one of the fabled swords of Careth, described in legends as "having the power to pierce the veils of reality." Before his untimely battle with lung cancer, Harold's grandfather often told her fantastic stories of how a long-forgotten tribe of humans had fought dark multiverse entities hellbent on crossing over. His descriptions were always vivid, tales of blood and heroic sacrifice against almost invincible foes whose actual nature defied the confines of flesh.

"Don't you think we should map out the rest of the network first?" Harold mumbled. "There may be yet other treasures to uncover."

"Picture. Now!" She repeated, holding the golden hilt in her right hand. "Do I look badass or what?"

"You certainly do..." He admitted as he reached for the compact digital camera. Though the lighting inside the chamber was poor, it didn't stop him from getting two or three big takes as she pretended to slay an invisible foe.

"All done. Come look."

"Eleanor sauntered to him, raven locks dripping over her long eyelashes. The sword was warm in her hands and far lighter than she expected. As she peered into the camera's screen, she let out a sudden shriek.

"What the hell is this?"

Harold's brows snapped together, prompted by bewilderment and fear. A shadow monstrosity of indiscernible shape swirled around the edge of the weapon, two glowing pools of infernal radiance calling out to them.

"Honey?" Eleanor muttered, the hairs on her arms and legs reaching for the unattainable sky. His expression dulled as hers hardened, features clouded by an evil spark.

It was really true - all of it! Unable to stop shaking, the late thirties wannabe explorer peed his pants when the ghastly figure in the picture enveloped his darling's once pristine smile in a web of festering decadence. Her neck spasmed, the brown tint in her irises slowly fading into whiteness.

"At last, a new host..." the thing History had tried its best to forget, hissed at him. The color drained out of his face as he let out a mortifying scream.

Slave Canvas

Oh, hello. Come closer. Closer... closer... okay, that's close enough. I know why you're here. You've come to me, hoping to have your thoughts turned upside down, your mind rewritten, reality altered to suit my every whim, isn't that right?

No? Are you sure? Well, that's interesting... usually I find my life, time, and inbox flooded with desperate pleas of wanting to be hypnotized by me. Men are such babies. They're all so eager to go down, drop deeper, and obey my every command... at least until their cocks explode and they suddenly forget they love me and worship the ground I walk on forever and ever. It would be nice if they admitted from the start they're just horny fucktards eager to shoot their load instead of wannabe slaves... God, I can't stand them!

Still there? Sorry for the rant, but you have no idea what it's like to deal with such idiots. So, what do you want, huh? To serve, and nothing else? You yearn to be useful to me because it's in your very nature to submit? Hmmm, yes... I can see that now. You have the eyes of a truly devoted, staring at a Goddess on Earth, completely blind to everything that isn't me. I like that. I like that a lot.

Okay, you have my attention, something which is incredibly hard to get and even harder to maintain, so how are you planning on doing that? Are you just going to keep on staring, latching on to my every word or are you indeed going to sink into them, find the hidden meanings each one conveys, until you're completely absorbed by them that you don't see a way out? Tell me, wouldn't that be the most wonderful feeling in the world?

I think it would. I think you think the same. I think you think the things I want you to think even when you're not sure you're thinking at all because thinking is hard. It's almost as hard as that thing you have between your legs. The funniest thing of it all is that you still believe it's yours, that you can do whatever you want with it after I stop talking but, if that were true, you would already be helplessly stroking like all the others instead of forgetting to do so. Human hands were designed for many things, most of them useful and noble. Pushing yourself to the brink of ecstasy is not one of them... unless I say it is.

So, devoted one... how will this play out? You say you don't want me to hypnotize you, yet you long to obey me without question. And I love my obedient pets even more when they're completely hypnotized and brainwashed. If you truly wish to please me, then you need to be open to the possibility of change, you need me inside your soul. There's no future for us unless you give me a room to stay within your innermost desires. I don't care how submissive you already are to me. Let me have it or leave. You have five seconds to give me the answer I wish to hear. Five, four, three, two...

giggles Easy, boy! Did I say you could kneel and kiss my feet? Did I tell you to take the heels of my leather boots into your mouth? Did I tell you that I adore that sort of worship and that is something I will train you for? No, and yet you're already triggered, dependent on the scenery I choose to paint in your slave canvas, locked inside the imaginary future that will forever paint itself as true. It's amazing what a couple of carefully constructed sentences can do...

Okay, I've had my fun, and It's obvious you can't wait for more of me. You can't, but you will. Patience will be your virtue, and my pleasure will never fade. Drop by tomorrow, boy. You're in for a treat.

The Interrogation

The early twenties African American woman sitting in the interrogation room had purple highlights running through her honey gold wig and what appeared to be a bubbly personality through and through. However, as a decade's worth of crime-solving history had taught him, Detective Paul Vance knew all too well how appearances could be deceiving. Case file in hand, he sat before her, his lower lip slightly twitching. It had been three hours since his last cigarette and the lack of nicotine intake was showing.

"Miss Walters," he began, thick Brooklyn accent coming out strong. "Before we start, do you have any inkling as to why I called you here?"

"No clue," the young beauty shrugged, a disdainful look on her otherwise sweet face. She was dressed in constricting dark-blue latex from head to toe, an almost full bodysuit save for the heart-shaped cutout to give her round breasts perfect room to breathe. "But this is the part where you're going to tell me, right?"

"We're here to talk about Brandon Myers." The Detective laid his hands on the cold, metal table.

"I'm sorry, who?" She raised a curious eyebrow.

"The name doesn't ring a bell? How about his alias, HighBud07, then?"

Her black eyes shimmered with recognition. "That one I do know. Brandon, you say? Curious, I always thought he had the voice of a Mike or something. Did he do something, officer?"

"That's Detective Vance, Miss."

"Goddess." She promptly corrected him.

"Excuse me?"

"Well, if you're so keen on using a title, I wish to be called by mine. That's Goddess Amber, Detective! Now what seems to be the problem? Please hurry because I've still got lots of things to do, today."

"Whatever they are, I'm sure they're not more important than an ongoing police investigation. Your file states you're a Hypnodomme, 'Goddess Amber'. Mind explaining to me what that means?"

"Why do you need me to explain it to you?" She smirked. "Are you thick or something?"

Detective Vance crossed his legs under the desk. "Indulge me, please."

"Fine! 'Hypno' is short for 'hypnosis' and 'Domme' is short for 'dominant'. I'm a dominant woman that controls her clients, submissives, and slaves through hypnosis and other mind-altering techniques. Easy of an explanation enough for you, Detective?"

"And why do you do that? Hypnotize people, I mean?"

"For money. For fun. Sometimes for both."

"Please state your connection to Mr. Myers then."

"You still haven't told me what this is all about..." She pouted.

"We'll get there in a minute. For the record, did you or did you not hypnotize Mr. Myers frequently in the last couple of months?"

"Highbud is one of my regulars, yes. He's into all sorts of kinky stuff that would probably make you blush, Detective. I would tell you all about them but a Domme and her pets have a privileged relationship, not so different from a doctor and her patients, you see?"

"Had a privileged relationship." He tapped the corner of the table and smirked back.

"Oh? Are you telling me he's dead?"

"Indeed. Funny thing about Mr. Myers... two days ago, he was filmed robbing a bank on 5th Avenue. Earlier in the morning, he was found, naked, with a single bullet shot wound at a friend's apartment, no sign of the money he stole. Even funnier is the fact that the last person he called from his cell phone before the robbery took place was one Goddess Amber Walters. Do you see where I'm getting with this?"

"I think I do, but that's one of the most ridiculous innuendos I've ever heard."

"And why is that?"

"Why would I hypnotize someone to rob a bank for me and then dispose of him knowing his recent contact history would immediately make me a prime suspect in the case?"

"That's what I'm asking you... 'Goddess'."

"I really don't know. I deal with fantasies every day, but you sure have a great imagination." She leaned on the table, giving him an unrestricted view of her DD breasts. "Do you have any evidence to support your delirious allegations?"

"Not yet, but..."

"... you'll send for me when you think you do, I'm sure." She pushed the table against his chest and stood up. "This was fun, but I said I'm busy. Goodbye, Detective."

"We're not done yet... 'Goddess'."

"I know my Constitutional rights so... yes, we are. Book a session if you want me to remove that stick up your ass or get you an even larger one for the weekend. You'll thank me when I'm done."

Never looking back, the Hypnodomme left the room, perky ass mocking his intelligence. Alone with his thoughts, Detective Vance pulled a cigarette from the back pocket of his tweed pants and sighed.

What I Need…

Diana strolled across the mall, husband Frank in tow. He was carrying in his hands the products of her latest shopping spree, bags full of expensive clothes and shoes she would most likely never use more than once, if at all. It didn't matter though; they would still look good in her walk-in closet and photo-ops mattered more than the consequences of maxing out credit cards. She was happy, but could be happier, still.

"Honey," she stopped to glance at him. "I just realized something. I seriously need a new purse - or ten! - to go with those shoes. You'll see to it, right?"

Frank, who was usually a kind-hearted and mild-mannered person even when he felt insulted, dropped the bags on the fake marble floor, cocked his head in disbelief and replied:

"Is that a joke?"

"Why would it be?" Diana retorted as if he had just insulted her in the worst way imaginable.

"Look at all this shit!" He gesticulated, furiously. "And besides, don't you have hundreds of purses already?"

"I do, but it doesn't matter. You're not listening to me, Frank! I said I need it and what I need..."

"... you always get." He muttered automatically, the fruits of a long-term conditioning blooming once again inside his mind. "Yes, dear. Of course."

"Mistress." She corrected him, a dark fire burning in her beautiful blue eyes. "You're going to pay for your insolence, Frank! Oh yes, you will!"

Later that day, she met her sister Natalie for lunch at their favorite Greek restaurant. Despite being the youngest of the two, Diana looked far from it, courtesy of a handful of cosmetic surgeries that had tried to perfect what really didn't it. Of all the adjustments, the nose job stood out the most, a small pink beak in an otherwise uniform visage. It was quite distracting and often the the subject of overused jokes, none of which the big spender was willing to endure.

"Not today, okay?" She said, dismissively.

"What happened?" Natalie queried, menu in hand.

"Everything!"

"Care to be more specific?"

"Frank questioned me. Again! It's the third time this month, Nat! I thought your hypnotic training was fool-proof!"

"It is." Natalie laid down the menu and looked her sister straight in the eyes.

"Then how do you explain his constant refusals to give me what I want? Having to trigger him all the time is annoying!"

"Have you stopped to consider that the training isn't the problem but rather the one using it?"

"So you're saying his disrespectful attitude is my fault?"

"I'm saying I've been doing this for about ten years now and no one has had any problems with my conditioning techniques except you. Not all people are tailored to be dominant, dear. It's possible you're one of them."

"That's absurd!" Diana grumbled.

"Is it? We both know you can be quite demanding, but what do you give him in return when he serves you the way you want to be served?"

"Nothing! Pleasing me should be gift enough. What I need, comes to be. What I say, goes!"

Natalie shook her head at her seemingly impossible naiveté. "Even the most well-trained horses need a carrot every now and then. You would do well to remember that."

"He doesn't need carrots. He just needs to obey. What do I do to ensure that?"

"I already told you how I think you should act. Take a step back, let him breathe instead of constantly nagging him. It will only make the conditioning stronger in the end."

"Yeah, not buying it! I'm not the problem, the training is. Not cool of you to teach me something you know it's flawed and then blaming me for not working. You need to do better than that, Nat!"

"And I need you to shut up right now."

"Huh?"

"Diana, I need you to shut up and what I need..."

"... you always get." The baby sister replied before committing herself to silence, unable to resist.

"Much better." Natalie remarked as she perused through the list of meat delicacies she loved more than anything in the world. There was nothing wrong with her training and there never would be. Diana just needed a reminder of that, and she had the perfect proof in mind.

Before the lunch was over, she decided she needed her kneeling under the table, tongue eager for a refreshment.

About the author

S.B., Simple Being, middle name Creative. Writer and artist with a penchant for themes of Femdom Hypnosis and Mind Control. His thoughts are his own except when they're not.

Besides indulging himself in kinky delights, he loves his furry family of two (dogs), sci-fi and horror stories, and puns galore. He's also been writing a piece of erotic micro-fiction every single day since January 1st, 2016 and has no intention of stopping anytime soon.

Find out more and keep up with his latest extravaganzas by visiting and supporting his personal website, Spell… B-O-U-N-D.

9 798676 527440